Balloons for Heaven

Written By Matt Chandler
Illustrated By Vicky Free

Zoliver Press
New York

To the Wells family
and all those who knew and loved Larry

Printed in the United States of America
ISBN-13: 978-0692229743
Balloons for Heaven/Chandler, Matt — First printing, June 2014
www.balloonsforheaven.com
www.mattchandler.net

Chloe was sad. Her mom and dad told her at breakfast that her hamster Mr. Wiggles was very sick.

They told her Mr. Wiggles had lived a great life. He was the best pet ever. But now, mom explained, it was time to let him go.

"Go where?" Chloe asked. Mr. Wiggles had lived in his cage in her bedroom for as long as she could remember. She didn't want him to go anywhere.

Chloe's dad explained that Mr. Wiggles was very old. When an animal has lived for a very long time, its body runs out of energy.

"Remember your pink speed racer?" her dad said. "When the batteries got old, the car couldn't go very fast, and then it just stopped working."

Chloe thought about that for a minute. She was sad when her racecar stopped working. Her grandpa had given it to her for her birthday. Then she remembered something.

"But you went to the store and got more batteries, and it worked like new again!" she exclaimed. "Can't you go buy some new batteries for Mr. Wiggles? Pllleeeaaassseee daddy."

Chloe's dad explained that animals and people don't run on batteries and that when they have lived a full life, it is time for them to go to heaven.

"Mr. Wiggles will be able to run around with lots of other hamsters and eat all of his favorite foods," he told her. "And he will have the biggest, fastest wheel to run on all night long!"

Chloe didn't really understand what heaven was, but it sure sounded like a nice place. If Mr. Wiggles couldn't be with her, at least he would be in a fun place.

"Can we go visit him Daddy?" she asked. "Can we bring him treats and watch him run on his new wheel?"

"Well, we can't go to heaven," her dad said, "because we still have our whole lives to live here on earth. But I'll tell you what we can do."

Chloe's dad went to the closet and came back with a bag of balloons, a piece of paper, and a crayon.

"How would you like to write Mr. Wiggles a letter and tell him how much you love him and miss him?"

"How does the mailman know where Mr. Wiggles lives?" Chloe asked. "Did you tell him that he moved to heaven?"

"We're not going to mail the note," her dad told her. He took the note she had written, carefully folded it in half, and tied it to a bright orange balloon that was left over from her brother Derek's birthday party.

"Let's go for a walk," he said.

It was a short walk to the park. Chloe was still trying to understand heaven. Her dad said it was a place where Mr. Wiggles would be happy and have lots of fun. And he could stay there forever. When they got to the park, her dad handed her the string of the balloon.

"I know you miss Mr. Wiggles sweetie," he told her. "So I want you to tell him how much you love him, close your eyes, and let this balloon go."

Chloe felt her eyes begin to fill with tears. She loved Mr. Wiggles so much. But she believed her daddy. She thought of her little hamster running on a giant wheel with lots of other hamsters, and it made her smile.

She slowly opened her hand and the string slipped away. It was a breezy day and soon the balloon, with her note, was sailing high in the sky. They watched it fly until it was a tiny speck and then, it was gone.

As Chloe and her dad walked back to their house she felt better. She still didn't quite understand why Mr. Wiggles had to leave. But at least he was in a happy place, and she could send him a letter any time she wanted.

Maddie didn't have a hamster, but she had the best daddy in the whole wide world. He could always make her smile. He worked in a giant toy store, and Maddie's favorite thing was to visit her daddy at work.

He loved to be silly and play with the toys. He was so much fun. He was like a giant kid to play with everyday!

But one day, something terrible happened. Maddie's dad got up really early for work at the store. Maddie was still asleep in her bed.

Her daddy was at work getting the store ready for all of the girls and boys to come shop. But he got hurt. They took Maddie's dad to the hospital, but even the best doctors couldn't help him.

It was his time to go to heaven.

When Maddie found out what happened, she didn't really understand. She just knew she wanted her daddy to come home and play with her. She loved it when he took her to the beach.

But her mommy explained that Daddy had gone to heaven. He had died. Maddie didn't know exactly what it meant to die. She knew that flowers died if it got too cold outside. She wondered if the flowers went to heaven too?

Her mommy explained that there are different reasons people go to heaven. She said that some people get very sick and their body can't take care of them anymore.

"But Daddy was strong and fast," Maddie thought to herself. "His body was great."

Her mommy told her that other people went to heaven because they got hurt very badly. But in Heaven God healed them and gave them angel wings.

That made Maddie feel a little bit better. She still didn't completely understand. But she liked the idea of her daddy being in a special place.

She knew about angels, and she smiled when she thought about her daddy flying around with his new wings.

She also knew her friend Chloe's hamster had died. She remembered her saying he was in heaven. Chloe told her heaven was a magical place. It was like one huge party.

It was a place where all of the best people and animals went when they died. And up in heaven everyone could look down and watch over their family and friends on earth.

That night, Maddie's mom was tucking her into bed. "Mom," she said. "Do you think Daddy is looking down from heaven watching me? That's what Chloe said happens."

"Absolutely," her mom told her, squeezing her hand. "Your daddy loves you more than anything, and just because he isn't here with us, he will never stop loving you. You will always be his little girl."

That made Maddie happy. She really wished her daddy could be here to take her to the park and go on the slide. She loved to go to the park with him. He was so much fun.

But then she remembered what Chloe said. Her daddy was watching her. And she remembered that Chloe had found a way to send her hamster Mr. Wiggles special letters when he went to heaven. She had an idea.

The next morning Maddie got up extra early. She got out her best crayons and some special paper. Her mom asked what she was up to. "I'm going to make Daddy a card to tell him how much I love him. And I want to send it to heaven!"

Maddie and her mom sat down at the table, and together they made the most beautiful note that had ever been written.

They drove together to the party store and bought the brightest balloon they had. The girl behind the counter explained to Maddie to hold onto the string tight or the special helium would make it float away.

"Oh, that's what I want," she told the clerk. "We are going to the park to send it to my daddy. He's in heaven."

The clerk told Maddie that was the best idea she had heard, and she told her that she bet her daddy would love getting a beautiful note and a bright balloon sent all the way from her.

At the park, Maddie and her mom found an empty bench to sit on.
They talked about her daddy. Her mommy reminded her about their trip to Myrtle
Beach and how much fun they all had. Maddie smiled.

Her mommy told her how proud her daddy was of her. How he was looking down
from heaven and he would watch her grow up into a beautiful young woman.

Maddie looked up into the bright blue sky. She couldn't see heaven, but she knew her daddy was up there.

She imagined he was looking down into the park. She raised her tiny hand and waved.

"I love you Daddy," she whispered. "I miss you."

Maddie and her mom watched until the balloon was just a speck in the sky. And then, it was gone. As they walked back to their car Maddie looked up at her mommy.

"Do you think Daddy likes his balloon?" she asked.

"I think he LOVES it sweetie," she told her. She bent down to give Maddie a big hug, and then they went home.

Made in the USA
Charleston, SC
09 June 2014